A Crimeless Christmas in Edgemont

Village of Edgemont, Volume 3.5

Della North

Published by Lynda French, 2024.

A CRIMELESS CHRISTMAS IN EDGEMONT

First edition. November 28, 2024.

Copyright © 2024 Della North.

ISBN: 978-1998074433

Written by Della North.

Table of Contents

With gratitude to my parents for making the Christmas holidays such happy occasions and the memories so special.

Preface

There's no lack of drama in Edgemont during the holiday season even without baffling deaths to unravel. Meet up again with your favourite couples as they navigate the season of goodwill.

If you're new to the *"Village of Edgemont"* mystery series you can read *"A Crimeless Christmas in Edgemont"* simply as a holiday story, but here's the background on our main characters:

Judith Taylor was a reserved woman in her early thirties living a solitary life with no family or friends until she unwillingly became involved in a police investigation led by Detective George Grant. Judith worked as the Bursar at the Edgemont School for Girls for several years but when Principal Patricia Johnson retires she recommends Judith as the replacement.

George Grant known as "Grant", fought his attraction towards Judith until a threat against her life pushed the two of them closer together. Although commitment-shy he is forced to recognize the depth of his feeling for Judith when another man takes an interest.

Lila Morelli, the Nurse at the Edgemont School for Girls, has steamrollered Judith into forming a friendship using her vibrant personality. Lila's marriage has ended and she's enjoying a flirtation with Brian Penner, the widowed father of a student at the school.

Brian Penner is a General Contractor with his own construction company. He met Lila when his daughter Beth went missing and her kindness drew him in. He's ready to commit to a serious relationship and wants to have a family with her.

Beth Penner Brian's daughter, a student at Edgemont School for Girls

Retirement Party

"Listen, I'm thrilled to bits that Marta Smith is retiring – especially since she's moving to BC – but why would I go to her farewell party? I can't stand the woman!"

"Judith! You can't go around saying stuff like that! Now that you're the principal you have to be more circumspect in your language."

It's Thursday evening and Judith is at the home of her best friend and coworker Lila Morelli. They've just finished a huge meal, courtesy of Lila's landlady Mrs. Piernitsky. While groaning on the couch, complaining they ate too much, Lila springs the retirement party news.

"Why? Pat never held back when she was principal. She hated Marta and said so."

"Look, just try to be a bit more um... diplomatic, okay?" replies Lila in a placating manner.

Grumbling, although she knows her friend is right, Judith adds: "Besides, Marta doesn't want me at her party. The only reason she's retiring is because I was chosen as principal over her so if I show up she'll accuse me of gloating."

"Oh we're not actually going to show up... sorry! is that what you thought I meant? No, we're attending virtually, via Zoom. We haven't been invited to the in-person event because there's a limit... I think it's a maximum of 15 people."

"Does Marta actually have 15 friends?"

"Apparently so! but seriously, she'd invite the cafeteria ladies if it meant making up her numbers to avoid inviting us."

"Works for me! So how do we go about this Zoom thing?"

"We'll join in using my iPad when they're giving her the group gift so she can thank everyone—"

"It will be like watching the Queen minus the little wave," interrupts Judith.

Ignoring her friend Lila continues: "...and then we just wish her well and sign off. Remember to watch what you say although I will be muting our microphone afterwards.

Judith frowns slightly as she thinks this over finally stating: "Right, I like the idea. Is there any way I can incorporate this Zoom into all of my future meetings, parties, dinners..."

"Aha! Now I know why you're so cranky," Lila smirks.

Judith squints her eyes and lifts an eyebrow.

"Never mind giving me that look, you're in a mood because you've got to go meet Grant's sisters. For a big family dinner." Lila starts to chuckle adding: "You can't Zoom into it, either."

"Ha-ha, but actually you're wrong. There's not going to be *a big family dinner* because that's no longer allowed. They figure this big surge in Covid hospitalizations occurred because of all the get-togethers at Thanksgiving so now the restrictions are back."

"Oh that's too bad. So you won't get to meet his family after all?"

"No I will, but it's just going to be his sisters. There's a thing about correct distancing and low, like only 30%, occupancy in restaurants so Grant and I are going to meet up with both of them for dessert. That was my idea. It's the shortest way I could think of for us to *get together for a meal* like they asked."

Lila shakes her head saying: "They're going to be your family too some day, you're going to have to get used to it Judith."

"Yeah well, I'll worry about that when *some day* rolls around."

Laughing at her friend's contrariness Lila says: "You're the one with the commitment problem, Judith. Grant's all-in with you two. It was such a big step for him to open up and admit to his guilt feelings in that college girl's death. He's changed so much, and all for the better."

"I know you were able to help him through that Lila, and we both appreciate it, but he does seem to be moving pretty quickly all of a sudden. I mean, first he wants me to meet his family and then he wants us to book appointments with a Realtor to view properties!"

"Oh really? that sounds great. This just goes to show that he's totally into you and the only drawback is you being such a pessimist."

"Well... that's not the only issue."

"What else?"

Biting her lip shows an uncertainty that's very unlike Judith's normal behaviour. Seeing that Lila is looking at her with caring sympathy Judith blurts out that she's not sure she's ready to become *Mrs. George Grant.* "I've hardly had a chance to be Principal Taylor and now I have to change my identity again?"

Accepting the nomination to be the school's new principal when Pat Johnson retired pulled Judith right out of her comfort zone. She's made great strides in the past year to overcome her natural shy reticence and Lila understands how Judith might think she's losing that achievement.

The nurse pauses for a moment to organize her thoughts. Lila's impulsive, bubbly personality draws everyone in but it's her thoughtful consideration when addressing serious issues that has earned her their trust and respect.

"You know I never once thought of Pat as *Mrs. Mark Johnson* instead of Principal Johnson. I don't believe changing your marital status will make a difference to anyone's perception of your ability to do your job. I realize once you marry most of the parents and folks in the community will assume you've become Principal Grant but you can always correct them if you plan to keep using Taylor."

"Won't Grant be offended if I don't change my name?"

"Judith! That's a question only Grant can answer but... to be frank, I have to say I think you're reaching for excuses. Look, I realize Grant has a strong will and personality but I don't believe for one minute that you'll lose your strength or sense of purpose simply by marrying. You still don't give yourself enough credit for what you've accomplished as the educated and intelligent leader of our school.

I understand that deep down inside you there's still that little girl pretending everything is okay while wearing unwashed clothes and going hungry but she deserves all kind of admiration and appreciation because she got you through it all."

Judith tears up as she gives her friend a hard hug. "Thank you, Lila. Thank you for your honesty and for making me feel good, too."

"My pleasure! Now, how about you allow yourself to consider that meeting Grant's sister might be fun and maybe you'll all become great friends, okay?

Anyways, paste a big smile on your face because it's time for us to log-in to Marta's celebration."

"What, that's now?"

"Yeah, and it should be well underway so I think we've stalled long enough. Heaven forbid we miss Marta's big farewell speech. Now hush, I'll mute it after we say our *hellos*."

Lila opens up her email and clicks on the *Join The Meeting* link. The site connects quickly and they immediately see two of their favourite teachers, Eddie and Tanya, who call out a warm welcome.

"We've just cut the cake but no one's getting a slice until Marta makes her farewell speech," complains Eddie just as all conversation drops so his words resound in the silence.

Lila quickly rescues the situation demanding that he hold up the cake so they can see it. Eddie calls out to Tanya and Joanne who lift the sheet cake explaining it's *Vegan Vanilla* and Judith chokes on a bark of laughter that she turns into a cough.

They can hear Marta in the background querulously asking *who's coughing? Is someone sick? Does somebody have Covid?*

"Can you tilt it so we can read the writing? the light's shining right on it," asks Lila ignoring Judith's whispered accusation *you're trying to make them drop it, aren't you?*

"Ah, that's better. I can read *Wishing you a Happy Retirement Head Teacher Marta*," announces Lila.

Marta's face suddenly fills the screen as she pokes her head in way too close and shouts: "Hello? Can you see me? Can you hear me?"

"Yes to both questions, Marta. Looks like you've got a good turnout for your party," says Lila.

Flattered, the woman visibly preens as she looks around at her guests.

"Is there anyone else attending via Zoom?" asks Judith. There's a bustle of conversation before Xiao's voice rings out saying *Pat and Mark Johnson are also due, in fact overdue, to check in.* A few moments later everyone can hear Pat's booming voice in greeting.

Lila replies: "Hi Pat, hi Mark. We're going to mute now so we can listen to Marta's speech."

"Wait, I can still hear them," says Judith worriedly.

"Well yes, we can hear them, but they can't hear us," explains Lila.

"Not a moment too soon!" declares Judith. "I mean *vegan cake???* I'm so glad I don't have to eat any of that!" Lila giggles in agreement.

The two settle back to listen to Marta's overly lengthy self-aggrandizing speech while interspersing their own commentary. Eventually the older woman wraps it up and Lila turns off the mute button so they can say goodbye and wish Marta a *happy retirement* and *good luck in her new home.*

Thieving Spree

Being the older of the two Reg does take liberties with his boss, and doesn't even bother to hide his chuckles at the expression on Grant's face while listening to a phone call. The senior detective is scowling as he barely squeezes out replies through his tightly pressed lips, and he's practically tearing the paper as he stabs his pen down taking notes.

Grant hangs up then picks up the handset again and smashes it up and down several times in a fit of pique. A buzzing sound a moment later signals an internal call coming in.

"This is Grant," announces the detective tersely.

Reg's chuckles turn into a belly laugh as he listens to half the conversation with Grant spitting out: "No, I didn't call the front desk. Well I can't help that. I don't know what happened. Okay... okay I won't. Bye."

Turning a baleful eye on his partner Grant explains: "Apparently we can call the front desk just by tapping this disconnect thingy repeatedly. Who knew?" and after another minute's thought he continues: "Who cares?"

"I'm guessing you've just had another complaint about stolen Christmas decorations, hmm?" Reg can't hide his smile.

"Honestly it's not like I want a murder or a robbery or a violent home invasion to investigate but having to deal with these irate citizens over these petty, bothersome misdemeanours... I mean, it's practically on a par with shoplifting. These rich people put their fancy blow-up decorations out on the lawn and then act all surprised when they get stolen."

"Rich people?"

"They must be! Would you spend $700 for a 20-foot inflatable Christmas tree to stick in your yard?"

"Does it light up?"

"Yeah it does, but—" Grant breaks off to frown at Reg when the older man starts laughing again, knowing his partner is teasing him.

Assuming a serious expression Reg asks: "How many is that now?"

Grant open a folder of reports shoved in any old way and starts flipping through the pages. "Hmm, it's about thirty lawn decorations from twelve or thirteen complainants. And let's see... the total value is hmm... actually it is getting pretty high considering these are just Christmas ornaments. The cheapest item is a 6-foot Grinch at $100 right up to the 20-foot tree that was matched with a 20-foot Santa so that homeowner's loss is about $1500."

"Hardly surprising that they've lost their Christmas spirit then," admits Reg.

"Normally I'd agree, but that call actually came from Hawaii. Yes, believe it or not, they're wasting their Hawaiian Christmas holiday time to phone in a complaint to me because their neighbour texted them about the theft. Sorry-not-sorry if I don't believe they're devastated by the loss."

"Are people allowed to fly south for vacations right now?"

"I don't think you can go to Mexico but yeah, we can fly Air Canada or WestJet to Hawaii with a negative COVID-19 test, no quarantining required. I remember reading about that a couple of weeks ago."

"Then I guess the next question is: how likely are those people to call our big boss to demand action?"

"Oh she's not going to take them seriously either. I mean yes, we'll all have to pay lip-service to addressing the problem, but those things have already been re-sold on a marketplace site and besides we have real crimes–" Grant cuts off his commentary there because in truth there are no *real* crimes happening in Edgemont right now. "I mean, I'm thankful, really, that things are quiet but–"

Reg interrupts to finish that sentence: "But you're frustrated because there's other stuff you want to be doing."

Grant thinks a moment before nodding as he explains: "You're right, Reg. That is my problem. It's not like I want anyone committing crimes, crimes always hurt somebody, but what I want to be doing is going out house-hunting and planning stuff with my sisters and buying Judith's ring and–"

"Wait, what? A ring?" Reg practically shouts out the question.

Grant twists his lips as if he can take back the words but then he sees that Reg is no longer teasing, the man is genuinely happy for him. In a deprecating manner Grant snarks: "What? no derogatory remarks about *the old ball and chain?*"

"Never! I think Judith is great. And hey, don't take this the wrong way Grant, but when a man as good-looking as you reaches your age without getting hitched well, people have to wonder what's wrong with you."

Grant expostulates but Reg keeps talking over him adding: "It sounds like I'm one of the first to be in the know so let me congratulate you, sincerely I wish you all the best."

Grant is much more than merely *good-looking,* and when he smiles unrestrainedly his face is startlingly handsome. Reg can't help but smile back at Grant's obvious delight but it doesn't seem right to ask a bunch of questions about *where?* and *when?* if Judith hasn't even heard the proposal yet.

Bringing the conversation back to business he states: "We should just be thankful we aren't suffering Calgary's epidemic of catalytic converter thefts."

Grant sits up straight exclaiming: "Don't tempt fate with comments like that, Reg. Those thefts are skyrocketing and the inhabitants of Edgemont are prime candidates since most are driving high-end SUVs, the easiest vehicles to steal from since the exhaust systems are so accessible."

"I read the stats and because it's such an easy job with a very lucrative payout it's become a serious problem. Who would have thought those parts would contain platinum and other costly metals?"

"And the victims do suffer: first, with a really loud, noisy car that's blowing black smoke out and venting noxious fumes in; then secondly, at having to pay for a replacement part."

"Yeah, and not only is that part expensive, but it's mandatory to have one. The article I read said it costs $2,000 for the average car and that price can run up to $18,000 for a bus."

"I never read anything about City busses or trucks being robbed... I guess they get parked overnight in lock-up yards. I did hear that a couple of salvage places were charged which is good because if the scrap dealers won't buy then no one will bother stealing to sell."

"Another good thing here is that most of our residents have garages where they can keep their vehicles safely inside.

Anyhow, I'll let you get back to your stolen outdoor decorations while I finish recording these tickets I had to write for snow-covered windshields and licence plates."

"Oh I'll bet you got some nasty complaints about those!"

Reg smirks but he's serious when he answers: "If someone can't spend two minutes to clean off their car for a safe ride then they shouldn't be driving, pure and simple. And I never stop to ticket just for a covered-up licence plate, if that's the only issue I only give them a warning. It's not about meeting quotas, no matter what the public might think."

Grant nods in agreement just as another internal call comes through. After listening Grant hangs up and now he gets to chuckle as he tells Reg: "It's your turn this time. Somebody's at the front desk complaining that their car's been stolen right out of their driveway and yes, you guessed it: they'd left it running to warm up."

The Unsavoury Boyfriend

Standing in the convenience store Beth idly flips through *The Jumbo Book of Crossword Puzzles* glancing at the titles on each page. It holds hours of brain-teasing challenges and she already knows she's going to buy it, but time is hanging heavily on her hands today. She's in no rush.

Hearing the cashier call out loudly she gives a guilty start as if she'd been caught reading one of the magazines on these shelves for free. But no, the complaint is directed at the guy standing in the doorway. It's because he's just standing there that the clerk admonishes him for *letting all the cold air in*. Although he doesn't acknowledge he's heard, the young man steps forward his eyes still staring at Beth.

Dusty sees a flawless face looking back at him. He first noticed strawberry-blonde hair shining brightly under the overhead lights. Florescent lights that usually colour people in sickly shades but not this girl. Nothing can dim her beauty. Dusty is lovestruck with all the power that emotion brings to a seventeen-year-old boy. He doesn't pause for one moment as he heads straight for her.

Beth is unable to move so she simply stands there clutching the book of puzzles. When the young man comes close she has to tilt her head back to meet his gaze. His eyes are a slate-blue, a colour she imagines comes from the very depths of the sea although she's never seen the ocean. Beth has been bit by the love bug too, and she's mesmerized by Dusty's presence.

Even the store clerk finds herself bemused watching the magnetic pull of attraction drawing the two young people together. She enjoys sharing their moment before giving herself a mental shake and querulously demanding: "I hope you're planning to buy that book that you're twisting and bending all over the place?"

Dusty gives an annoyed frown at the interruption but Beth hurries over to pay at the counter. She's flustered and first says *no,* then *yes,* to buying a plastic bag. She's already pocketing her change by time Dusty belatedly reaches for his wallet but that's just as well since he has very little cash in it. Completely forgetting whatever brought him into the store in the first place he turns to escort Beth out.

"I'm Dusty, Dusty Matthews."

"Oh! Hi, Dusty. I'm Beth, well Bethany, but I go by Beth–" she replies with a faint blush before he interrupts her asking: "Why? I mean, Bethany is a really pretty name."

When Beth just stares at him, her shy smile reflected in her eyes, Dusty continues: "A really pretty name for a really pretty girl."

Beth's pupils dilate and her mouth widens into a big smile. Her cheeks now bloom with bright colour as she breathily whispers: "Thank you."

The slew of feeling that rips through Dusty's body and mind is too much. He can't utter a word but he needs to reach out. He takes hold of her hand and clasping it tightly they start walking with no particular destination in mind. Comfortable with the silence they just enjoy each other's company.

Finally Dusty says: "I have a car if you want to go for a ride?"

"Oh I can't. I have to help serve at *Feed the Hungry* tonight with my Dad. Soon, actually. But otherwise.." shyly she ducks her chin down.

"I'll call you tomorrow then, eh?"

"Umm, yeah but Dusty I, uh... um..." Beth's mind is casting about wildly trying to say the right thing without sounding too young and giving away her age. She won't be sixteen until January.

Beth realizes that she likes Dusty a lot and doesn't want to make a bad impression. She recognized him right away but they've never actually met.

"You don't want to go out with me," he says with disappointment, making it a statement not a question.

"I do but... I really um... I don't think I'm allowed to date yet. It's never come up actually, but my Dad is..." she trails off miserably but Dusty's face brightens.

"You can ask him–"

"Maybe we should just meet somewhere like, um, back at the mini mart again?"

"Yeah, sure! What time?"

Beth is so happy seeing how eager Dusty is. They settle on a time but she warns she'll have to be home in good time for dinner with her Dad and his girlfriend.

"That's okay, I'll have to grab a couple of hours sleep before my shift anyhow."

"You have a job?" she's visibly impressed and Dusty can't help boasting a little.

"Part time, but I can get more hours if I want them. I work the late shift unloading trucks and stocking the shelves at Superstore and it pays pretty good."

"Isn't that hard with school?"

"I'm not the greatest student. I skip a lot." Dusty is hiding a motherlode of teen angst behind that truancy claim but he likes Beth and he doesn't want to reveal anything that might put her off.

She's oblivious to his dilemma and earnestly states: "But you've got to graduate, you need a diploma. I'm good in school, maybe I can help you?"

He eagerly agrees saying: "Yeah, okay, that would be good."

They exchange smiles, happy to be making plans together.

Visiting Calgary Zoo

Judith and Lila are enjoying an unexpected free afternoon at the Calgary Zoo. The sky is overcast and dull but the temperature is a seasonable 3°C.

Since the Alberta Government ordered the closure of Grades 7 to 12 at the end of November it made sense to shut down all of Edgemont School for Girls. So the two women decided to come see the animals and catch up with each other's news.

They'll also take this opportunity to discuss the online learning programmes that are available. With less than a month's worth of classes left for this semester the focus will be less on teaching and more on entertaining the students.

"Mark Johnson agreed to make a video of him reading *A Christmas Carol* for the older kids and *How the Grinch Stole Christmas* for the younger ones. Pat told me it's turned out perfectly, he's got such a marvellous voice."

"That's a wonderful idea and I have a surprise for you, too. I videotaped Mrs Piernitsky doing some traditional Ukrainian baking. She's made a Christmas bread, Kyiv cake, honey cake, and other stuff I can't pronounce but it's delicious. I told her to just chat away exactly like she did when she had us both over to learn how to make cabbage rolls, remember? and it worked great. She's a natural.

She explains each step as she handles everything in her unhurried way and you'd think you were watching a professional cooking show on TV. The children will love listening to her even if they don't understand half of what she's saying. They'll just enjoy having a real old-fashioned grandma talking to them. I've written out the recipes as well for any families who want to try making the desserts themselves."

"Lila that's brilliant! I'm going to want those recipes too. Grant loves Mrs Piernitsky's cooking."

"Everyone does. Every time I come home I practically swoon for the first minute inhaling the glorious aromas."

"I talked to a couple of teachers about driving two carloads of choir singers around to perform outside both of the care homes here, and in the hallways at the hospital. Eleanor Frampton got all the necessary authorizations for that. I have a feeling we'll get more than enough volunteers so we might be able to do a couple of performances."

"Sounds like you're well-prepared and have everything in hand. We re-open to all grades on January 11th, right?"

"That's right, and now that we've discussed our school business let's enjoy our visit here. It's perfect weather for the Penguin Walk," states Judith.

"Oh I want to see that," enthuses Lila. "I love penguins, just looking at them makes me laugh, what time does it start?" She looks adorable in a fisherman's knit bobble hat with a matching scarf and mitts.

"I don't think it's on right now because of the restrictions. It would have been in the morning, anyhow."

"Oh, well that's disappointing. Um, why did you mention it?"

Judith laughs a bit sheepishly saying she's sorry she got Lila's hopes up. "It's just that the Penguin Walk is a popular thing in Calgary and I thought you knew about it. It's weather-dependent so usually anyone planning a trip to the zoo in wintertime wonders if the temperature will be right," she explains.

"What happens during the walk?"

"It's more of a waddle and it is hilarious. Here, we're at the penguin enclosure and look there are a couple outside. I love how they all turn to stare in the same direction at the same time even though there's nothing to see."

"The meercats do that too."

"Yes that's right, but their home is indoors and I'm not sure if the Savannah building is open. Anyhow, these penguins do mosey along but they can move quite quickly when they want, and there's always one or two who stray. The bystanders are warned in advance not to reach out or touch, I think they might bite—"

"The bystanders?"

"Oh ha-ha. Anyhow, several keepers escort about a dozen penguins as they walk from their enclosure to that bridge down there," she points to the wide paved bridge over the Bow River. "And then back. It's good exercise for the birds plus it gives them an interest, a bit of excitement.

I've seen it twice now and you can't help but laugh watching them. But the thing is the audience is all huddled together behind a rope barrier and that won't work with social distancing."

"Well this Covid can't last forever and I'm just glad the zoo is open."

"Yeah, we won't get the full experience with so much indoor stuff closed but I kind of like buying the tickets online – no line-ups – and having designated times. We don't have to worry about it getting too crowded."

"Yet the parking lot was crowded. Especially with having to leave an empty parking stall between each car." Judith had driven the two of them there having registered her license plate to pay for parking when she bought the tickets. Naturally Lila was paying her back half the cost.

"Mmm, but this is also a paid parking lot for the C Train to downtown so probably most of those cars don't belong to zoo-goers."

Lila links her arm with Judith's telling her to lead them since she knows her way around. The layout of the Calgary Zoo lets visitors see lots of animals without having to walk long distances, although from one end to the other is quite a trek in the cold weather.

The walking areas are widely spaced and in front of each exhibit the required six-foot zone is marked by animal paw prints.

"That's a cute idea using wolf prints," comments Judith.

"That's bear, not wolf."

"It can't be, the claws aren't long enough," argues Judith.

"I didn't say it was a grizzly–"

Interrupting Judith complains: "Oh Lila, you'll argue over anything."

Her friend's chuckle sounds suspiciously like a giggle when she replies: "That's what Brian says!"

Smiling back at her Judith teases: "Sooooo how are things going with you two?"

"Really well, actually. The three of us make a happy little family."

"Beth is a great girl." Judith almost mentions that she saw Beth earlier but for some reason she holds back. Well, not some reason, she admits to herself silently, but because of that boy the girl was with.

"She really is. I'm sorry for her though because all these restrictions, and keeping apart, is awfully hard on the young people. It's like they're losing a year of their lives because of having to stay indoors so much. No social life, in fact almost no in-person interactions at all. It's so unfair to them, especially not being able to go anywhere locally or on vacation."

"Well I wouldn't want to be trapped on a plane with who knows what germs floating around right now anyhow," says Judith with a shudder.

"Actually this would be the best time to travel because every other seat has to be empty. No talkative person or big grump sitting in the adjacent seat. And apparently the air circulating in the cabin is like pure oxygen or something."

"So they say." Judith's tone is skeptical even though she's never actually flown. She's never taken a train or been on a boat, either.

"The hockey players are all flying up to play in Edmonton. It's a hub or a bubble or something, and considering how much money they get paid the owners must believe it's perfectly safe or they'd never risk it."

The women get distracted from their conversation by the antics of the Red Pandas. They stop to watch the active animals enjoying the cooler weather as they somersault up and over their climbing apparatus.

"These little guys are cute but they kinda remind me of the raccoons we had back in Toronto. Everyone hated them for all the trouble they cause. I swear they can open anything so no type of garbage can is safe."

"We don't have them here."

"Uh yeah, we do. Raccoons live everywhere in Canada."

"Not in the Rockies. Don't ask me why it's just one of those little factoids I learned."

"Really? Maybe there's a predator native to the mountains that keeps them away. I hope that's right because they can be quite vicious and carry rabies as well. Anyhow, these Red Pandas are cute, but let's go see the real Pandas."

"The Giant Pandas aren't available either. They're in quarantine before they go back home to China so no, we can't see them."

"So no Penguin March, no Giant Pandas, and look here this sign says *Flamingos* but it's empty."

"Lila it's November, of course the flamingos aren't out. Did you not visit the Calgary Zoo website like I told you to? then you'd know what's going on here.

Listen, you can see several types of bears, musk ox, bison, moose and deer, foxes, wolves, snow leopards, mountain lions, real lions, tigers, giraffes... well no, maybe not the giraffes."

"Okay, okay I get it and I'll stop bitching. And thank you for bringing the water and snacks, it never occurred to me that we wouldn't be able to buy stuff here. Like hot chocolate, which would go really good right about now. I figure the mark-up must be a huge portion of the income earned from zoo visits."

"You're probably right because stuff like bottled water isn't cheap but, again, the website explained the *snack shacks* are closed."

"Yeah, yeah, yeah I get it. Next time we plan on doing something together I'll complete my homework assignment first," teases Lila rolling her eyes. Judith can't help but laugh along although she is irritated at what she sees are complaints against her beloved zoo.

"Don't mind me, now. Besides, I'm here to spend time with you, Judith. Seeing the animals is a bonus."

"Aww, every time you get me frustrated enough to scream you turn around and say something nice and all is forgiven."

"Huh! Brian says that too!" Lila laughs. "So this really has been quite a year, eh?"

"A lot of firsts, for me and... oh Lila take that smirk off your face. There are other *firsts* you know! Like this is the first time Calgary didn't have Stampede and July felt really empty without it."

"You do surprise me, Judith. I have to say I wouldn't have pegged you as a regular at the rodeo."

"Me? seriously? No, but I did attend one time, last year actually, on the 100th anniversary. I had no interest in the rides or anything on the midway well, except for those little cinnamon doughnuts? So good! But I did check out all of the displays and shows in the buildings and they were impressive. Everything from western-themed oil paintings to massive handmade quilts, and all the baby animals, too.

I saw a show, not the Amazing Dogs or whatever it's called because that line-up went forever, but something... nope, can't remember but I know I really enjoyed it at the time. I've never been to the rodeo portion but maybe someday?"

"Grant doesn't strike me as a Stampede-goer either."

"No, I expect you're right about that except he did grow up here so he's probably been many times."

Opening a packet of salted peanuts, a favourite snack she can never indulge in the school environment because of people's allergies, Judith is reminded again of what, or rather who, she saw when she stopped at the convenience store to pick up their supplies.

She's already passed up on one chance to mention it to Lila because something is holding her back. She wants to think over what she witnessed and try to figure out in her own mind how it struck her before discussing it.

Pulling into the parking-lot for a quick stop before going on to pick up Lila Judith recognized Beth when she spotted the girl's familiar rose-coloured coat. As Judith parked she planned to call out a *hello* but by time she got out of her car Beth was walking away in the company of a young man. Not someone Judith knew and based on how he looked he was someone she would be very unlikely to know.

Judith wears prescription glasses when driving so she can easily read street signs although Edgemont is such a small community she isn't likely to get lost.

Having the glasses on enabled her to get a good profile view of the fellow. A glint of something shiny that must be a dangling earring peeked between the strands of purpley-black hair and Judith was certain she could see the ink markings of a tattoo reaching up to his neck. He wore a leather jacket over a black hoodie, blue jeans, and cowboy boots.

Thinking over what she observed earlier Judith struggles over whether or not to say anything to Lila. She recalls that the guy was tall and broad-shouldered but lanky with a lot of growing to do to fill out his frame.

His appearance was slightly alarming but at least he seemed to be Beth's age or just a year or two older. Not a young man but a youth, another teenager. Beth attends an all-girls school so he can't be one of her classmates but maybe his sister is? or he might be an acquaintance from The Centre, the Edgemont Activity Centre?

Judith decides to keep quiet for now but she'll sound out Grant for an opinion when he comes over for dinner tonight.

Dilemmas

Grant has to leave in about half-an-hour but right now he and Judith are relaxing on her couch, stuffed full after enjoying a satisfying meal of comfort food.

She had a beef roast and root vegetables slowly cooking in her crock-pot while out for the day with Lila. As soon as Grant came into the apartment he breathed in the tasty aroma and embracing Judith whispered in her ear: "Oh so you *do* know that the way to a man's heart is through his stomach, hmm?"

"Actually, the quickest way is through his chest with a butcher's knife," quips Judith adding, "At least, that's what I've heard!"

Grant kisses her lightly before warning that if he wasn't so hungry he'd be investigating her surprising *and worrying* bloodthirsty side. Laughing, Judith takes his coat and sends him through to the dining-room but he goes straight to the kitchen to help her carry out their plates.

Finding him ready to lend a hand she teases: "You really are hungry!"

Grant hasn't eaten since breakfast and Judith has a good appetite after spending hours walking around at the zoo. They both concentrate on their food before settling in the living-room for coffee and a chat. Grant slips his arms around Judith pulling her near but keeping enough distance to look into her face as he asks: "What's on your mind, sweetheart? You're a million miles away."

"Oh I... I do have something I'm struggling with. You know Grant, I try not to repeat my mistakes and what I've been thinking about is how sometimes keeping quiet can cause even more trouble, right?"

"Honey I don't know what you mean. Keeping quiet about what?"

He wants to help but he has no idea what she's talking about. Judith frowns as she exhales noisily. Grant can see that she's really bothered by whatever it is. Smoothing her hair back from her forehead he catches her eye and holds her gaze.

"Remember last December, when it came out that I'd witnessed an interaction that wasn't my business so I didn't mention it to anyone but it could have impacted the police investigation?"

Grant takes a moment to untangle the sentence and to think back to the events of last year's murder. That's when he met Judith and his mind wanders while he recalls the first time he saw her.

"Grant?"

Brought back to the here and now he smiles to think that the woman in his arms was once so cold and distant. So much has changed in the past year. "I was just thinking that's when we met and I had no idea then that we'd be here together now."

Smiling back Judith agrees that she'd never have believed it either. "But okay, I'll tell you what's going on. I saw Beth Penner in the company of a boy and he was... well, not very satisfactory."

"What exactly does that mean?"

"I mean he's a certain type, an unsavoury type. Leather and tattoos, dyed hair, and an earring."

"Oh, I see." As a policeman Grant understands what worries Judith.

"So I'm wondering if I should say something? except it's really none of my business! And who would I talk to: Beth? Brian? Ugh, I can't do that."

"Judith without knowing a thing about him, just from what you've described, I have to say he sounds like trouble and Beth doesn't need a boyfriend like that."

"I don't know about him being a boyfriend... what if he's just an acquaintance? I don't want to stir up trouble. I mean, they weren't um, necking, or anything like that so..."

"Judith, you're the principal of a girl's school and you need to know how to deal with situations like this."

Stung by his comment Judith retorts: "I do know how!"

Grant calmly replies: "I realize that, so what's the problem here?"

Judith's indignation flees and her voice quiets as she explains: "I guess it's different because I have an attachment to Beth–"

Gently Grant interrupts saying: "Exactly, and that should make your decision even easier."

* * *

While Judith and Grant are discussing her dilemma Reg is indulging in his practice of driving around and keeping an eye out. As usual he includes the Edgemont Trailer Park in his list of areas to check up on.

Following the 15 km speed limit signs he slowly cruises through the complex of mobile homes and is pleased to see that most of the residents have put up Christmas decorations.

He's just thinking how festive the coloured lights and fir wreaths are when he turns a corner and in the common area sees a truly impressive display of huge inflated figures. *There's Mickey and Minnie Mouse, and the Grinch and his dog um... Max! that's it, and that tree has got to be twenty feet high and uh-oh,* he thinks. *These match the descriptions of those stolen outdoor decorations that have been plaguing Grant.*

Reg, for so many years a man who saw everything in terms of black and white, good and bad, right and wrong, has mellowed in his thinking now that his own kids are kids no longer. He's had some real eye-opening discussions with his adult children, enough that he now finds himself in a quandary.

It used to be that what he should do and what he wants to do would be the same thing, no question, but now? Now he's thinking about someone holidaying in luxurious accommodations 3,000 miles away and not missing their decorations while lower-income folk are delighting in a wondrous spectacle. A real Christmas treat.

And he knows that as a policeman he should most definitely not be thinking those thoughts at all.

* * *

Grant sighs at his own inability to escape policeman-mode. He was reluctant to leave Judith and the warmth of both her apartment and her kisses but shopping access and hours are restricted so he's at the mall. To date he's been unsuccessful on his quest to find an engagement ring that will suit his girl.

However, even though he's on his own time he can't turn a blind eye to crime. *Or rather almost-crime,* he thinks with a sigh. He spotted the two girls right away, it's impossible to miss the very obvious signs of nervous teenagers planning to shoplift. Looking around he sees that all the store clerks are busy with other customers so he decides to show a little seasonal goodwill.

Sidling up alongside them he flashes his badge and gets panic-stricken gasps in response.

"Put everything back and go. Consider this an early Christmas present... and a warning."

Both of them drop the earrings clutched in their hands. One of the girls tries to bluster that she's gift shopping for her mother's present but the other whispers a fervent *thank you Officer!* and grabbing her friend's elbow drags her away.

Seeing them leave an older woman hurries over and she breathes out a relieved sigh when she spies the gold jewellery scattered on the counter.

Grant's good looks rarely go unnoticed and as soon as they finish with their customers two other women come over to assist him.

The first woman tells them *I've got this* and turning to Grant introduces herself as Elizabeth, the store manager, adding: "And I owe you a discount for your help. I saw the look on those girl's faces and noticed the badge in your hand so thank you for that. We're too busy to go through the hassle of arresting shoplifters, and no one wants to ruin anybody's Christmas."

"I appreciate the offer, Elizabeth. My name's Grant, by the way. I'm looking for an engagement ring but... I should probably pay full price in case she doesn't like it and I've got to bring it back."

"Returns aren't a problem Grant, but let's pick something perfect to save you an extra trip. We'll start with you telling me a bit about your *fiancee*. How old is she? how would you describe her style of dress? and what type of work does she do?"

Smiling at Elizabeth's confidence that Judith will say *yes* when he proposes Grant takes a moment to picture his love. The happy look on his face has the other store assistants sighing. "Judith is the new principal at Edgemont School for Girls. She's... actually I don't know how old she is. She must have had a birthday since I've known her because we met a year ago. Hmm, I'll have to find out... I can't believe I don't know! But I'm going to guess early thirties. She graduated university and worked in her job as school bursar for quite a few years so yeah, that would be about right. She looks younger but dresses older if that makes sense?"

Elizabeth is nodding in understanding. After thinking for a moment she moves to a cabinet which she unlocks and chooses four rings, placing them on a black velvet cushion. Presenting her selection to Grant his gaze zooms in on one ring and he knows it's the perfect choice. His brilliant smile has all the women in his vicinity beaming right back at him.

An Early Christmas Present

Judith is flustered when Grant calls to say he's downstairs to pick her up and they need to go right away. They hadn't made plans to go out today so she wonders what this is about and hopes everything is okay.

Having just got home from work she's still wearing her business attire. Quickly fluffing her hair she puts her coat and boots back on then grabbing her purse and keys she hurries out the door and down to her building's front entry.

Grant is standing at the passenger door of his car ready to seat her which he does without answering any of her questions. He's got the car nice and toasty because he knows Judith feels the cold. She wears boots long before the snow starts falling in order to keep her feet and ankles warm.

Once he pulls out of her driveway and onto the road he starts talking. "I'm hustling you along because we have a very small window of opportunity and when I got the call I grabbed it."

Smiling at her puzzled expression he explains: "I want to get you a cat for Christmas and a female kitten is available for you to look at and decide. If you don't like her please say so and we'll wait until we find the perfect pet. It's not a problem at all.

The pet store has a waiting list because Covid isolation has driven up demand, especially for kittens. She's not a newborn, she's three months old, and she's a rescue from a drug house. She's been checked over by a vet and is perfectly healthy."

"Grant... oh! this is... wow!"

"I know, eh? I honestly didn't think I'd be able to get a cat for you this Christmas. So strange because it used to be people were always trying to offload unwanted kittens.

I mentioned that when I first spoke to them at the pet shop and the lady said having a bylaw preventing cats from roaming freely caused a big drop in the cat population and, I guess not surprisingly, an increase in the number of squirrels, and of course birds.

So, since cats can only go outdoors on a leash far less are being taken to the Animal Shelter nowadays. Which is good unless you're trying to acquire a cat while working against a deadline."

"Oh Grant this is so nice of you! A cat, a kitten. I'm sure I'll love her."

"Well honestly if you don't it's okay, as I said if that's the case we'll just keep looking. It's really important that the two of you bond so if she isn't the one then it just wasn't meant to be. Anyhow, we're almost there and time-wise we're good."

Judith sees that they're at a big chain pet store and people with dogs on leashes are going in and out. Grant parks and they quickly walk inside. Now Judith feels anxious that someone else will try to get *her* cat.

Grant recognizes the woman he spoke to when he came in three weeks ago and soon she's asking people to step back six feet from the cat area so they can see the kitten. A tiny black-and-white dynamo is leaping from one end of her enclosure to the other. She must be chasing dust motes or maybe ghosts because the humans can't see anything.

The store clerk reaches in and before Judith knows it she and the kitten are nose-to-nose. A rough little tongue darts out to give a lick and Judith instantly falls in love. She snuggles the cat to her chest with a happy sigh feeling it purr.

"I'm guessing it's a *yes*," Grant tells Donna, the woman serving them, and Judith nods sharply, already fiercely protective of her kitty.

After completing several pages of an adoption contract and watching Grant spent a shocking amount of money they leave the store with Judith carrying her pet in a travel case and Grant wheeling an overladen shopping cart full of everything any cat could possibly need.

On the drive home he asks: "What are you going to call her?"

"I don't know I... hmm, she's certainly a pretty little thing and look! her markings are perfectly symmetrical." Judith is studying the kitten inside the carry-case. It's mewing at them as it twists and turns to explore this new environment.

"Yes Donna said this little one is *pure tuxie* which means she's a Tuxedo cat because of the black-and-white colouring."

"But the paperwork says she's a Domestic Shorthair."

"Yeah, that's the breed but her category, I guess, is Tuxedo."

After tilting her head from one side to the other as she considers the cat Judith announces: "I'm going to call her Panda."

"That's cute."

"Not just because she's black-and-white–"

"No, I get that," he interrupts, "Or else you'd call her Penguin."

"Penguin!? That's a dumb name for a cat, Grant! No, she's Panda because of her colouring *and* because she's a little roly-poly bundle of fur. She's perfect and I love her!"

Looking at his girlfriend with her face aglow and her eyes shining Grant swallows a lump in his throat before replying: "That makes sense Judith, because you're perfect and I love you."

Her cheeks blush to an even rosier hue as dimples appear. "Oh Grant," she smiles.

"Let's get this little one introduced to her new home and all her gear set up. You'll have to decide where you're putting the litter-box, her climbing-scratching-whatever thingy, and her bed. Maybe feed her right away too. That will reassure her."

"Grant I was so surprised to read that note in the paperwork about not giving her milk. I thought all cats love milk?"

"I'm sure they do, but it isn't good for them. Once they're weaned from Mama Cat they only need water to drink. Milk is fattening and it can be hard to digest."

"Well I want to do everything exactly right so no milk, in fact no people food at all."

"I'm sure she'll be hard to resist, but it's for her own good. By the way did the paperwork say anything about chocolate?"

"It did! It said chocolate is harmful, possibly poisonous, same for grapes and raisins – although they don't know why – lilies and other plants too, but I don't have any so that's not an issue. Oh! that reminds me, you better spend the night tonight so she gets used to your presence in the apartment."

Once they arrive at Judith's place Grant leans in towards Panda in her carry-case and stage-whispers: "Good job kitty-cat, you're on Team Grant already!"

A Family Get-together

Grant is enjoying a cup of Judith's excellent coffee while sitting at the kitchen table watching Panda try to scale his leg by digging her sharp little claws into the fabric of his pants.

Once she gets to his knee he gently swings his leg back and forth giving the kitten a ride. She looks up at him in wide-eyed surprise and he realizes it took less than 24 hours for this tiny girl to steal his heart.

He smiles at the memory of last night's bedtime when Judith set up the kitten's bed in the living-room only to have to move it to the bedroom floor and then to keep moving Panda from their bed to her bed. After this happened several times Judith gave in and cleared a space for the cat-bed on her night-table.

Panda seemed to settle, but Grant woke during the night when a furry tail tickled his nose and he discovered a purring bundle of fluff tucked into Judith's neck.

Hearing his sister's ringtone on his phone Grant smiles as he rudely answers: "Make it quick, I'm busy entertaining a kitten."

"Too much information little brother. I'm calling to say we're both free today if you two can meet up about 1:00?"

"That sounds great. I don't have to go in to work until later and we don't have anything else planned. The Cheesecake?"

"Where else? We're looking forward to meeting *Kitten*."

"Hah! the kitten in question is actually a real cat. Judith and I will be there, bye!"

Although the call only lasted a few minutes by time it finished Panda had reached Grant's lap and curled into a ball. Entering the kitchen Judith stops at the sight of Grant and Panda together and after saying *awww* she aims her phone and takes a photo.

Her smile turns into a worried frown when Grant tells her about the phone call saying they'll all be getting together today.

"Today! Why? I mean, what's the rush?"

Grant is puzzled until he realizes Judith is nervous and that thought strikes him as funny. His sisters have been playing matchmaker for so many years now that he's sure they'll be more than willing to welcome anyone he chooses. They can't wait to meet Judith.

Scooping up Panda into one hand he reaches out with the other and pulls Judith into his lap. While she takes hold of the kitten Grant cuddles her against his chest. Bestowing a kiss he reassures her that there's nothing to worry about.

"But what if–"

"But nothing, sweetheart. I know my sisters will love you almost as much as I do."

"Oh but what about Panda?"

"What about her? What do you mean?"

"We can't leave her alone!"

Chuckling Grant says: "Of course we can. She'll probably sleep the entire time we're away. Besides, we don't have a choice, it's not like we can take her with us."

"But what if she gets into something, into trouble somehow, and we're not here? What if there's a fire in the building?"

"Oh honey now you're just being ridiculous–"

Judith struggles to free herself from Grant's hold angrily snapping: "Oh I'm ridiculous, am I? Ridiculous for caring about the well-being of this helpless little kitten–"

In a determined voice and with firm hands pulling her back down onto his lap Grant interrupts saying: "Yes, you are because Judith you know perfectly well one of the reasons you wanted a cat is because they're the perfect house pet. Self-contained, independent little creatures that enjoy their own company.

Now admit it, the real problem is that you've worked yourself up about meeting my family and I've told you repeatedly there's nothing to be alarmed about. My sisters are excited to meet you and I'm sure you'll like them so stop worrying, okay?"

Judith is anxiously chewing on her bottom lip and Grant thinks she looks adorable.

Brightening up as an idea strikes her she suggests maybe she can get Beth Penner to cat-sit Panda while they're out."

Grant thinks it's silly but knows better than to voice that opinion. Instead he asks with a barely restrained laugh: "You seriously want to hire someone to look after your cat for a few hours?"

"Yes! Panda's just a kitten and this place isn't child-proofed never mind kitten-proofed."

"Then by all means, call Beth and see if she can come over by say twelve-thirty?"

"Oh Grant I know you think I'm over-reacting but..."

He gives her a squeeze before letting her go make the phone-call and replying: "Whatever makes you happy."

He just loves seeing Judith's care and devotion towards the cat. *What a great mother she'll make* he surprises himself by thinking.

* * *

Several hours later, after Beth has arrived to meet Panda and receive instructions along with both of their phone numbers, Judith reluctantly says goodbye and she and Grant head out for their dessert social meeting.

Hearing his name called as soon as they enter the cafe Grant strides forward with a big grin on his face. There are two women looking towards them and one half-stands to wave. He finds that he's yanking on Judith's arm so he turns back to see why she stopped. She hurries, smiling, not wanting to show her reluctance.

He studies her a moment before leaning in close to say: "Don't be shy, sweetheart." Judith is both relieved that he understands and annoyed that she's so transparent.

It's glaringly obvious that the three people standing here now are closely related. The sisters both share Grant's fair colouring although their blonde hair is golden to his near-white shade, and they all have the same pale blue eye colour. Judith didn't know the women were twins.

"Judith, these are my much older sisters Lady and Gail," he smirked as he introduced the women.

"Lady? that's uh... unusual–"

"It's Adelaide, actually, Addy for short, and Abigail, known as Abby to everyone but her brother. George has always been difficult."

Grant rolls his eyes at that remark but Judith joins right in with the sisters saying: "Oh I understand perfectly! and I agree with what you've said about Grant, I mean you both look far younger than him."

Grant always teased that he's the youngest child because his parents stopped having children after they got the boy they always wanted. His older sisters would complain to their mother who'd reassure them by saying *we stopped because we were afraid of what might come next!* Usually one of his siblings would then give him a pinch or a slap. At a year-and-a-half younger he never found it easy to fight back against the girls.

Since their father was usually away, travelling on business, Grant reveled in his role as the bratty boy in an otherwise all-female household. He now turns to Judith with his mouth dropped open in surprise while his sisters laugh claiming simultaneously, *we like her* and *finally! you've met your match.*

"How about this then: I'll call you guys Addy and Abby if you call me Grant, deal?"

His sisters are still pretending to mull over his suggestion when a middle-aged server wearing a face mask comes out with a whiteboard listing the day's offerings. Menus don't get passed around any more.

Judith's comment of *I'm glad they have other desserts because I don't like cheesecake* is greeted by shocked silence. It is, after all, a cheesecake restaurant chosen because it's been a favourite of the Grant siblings for their entire lives.

Grant's dismay is evident in the way he clears his throat but Judith isn't cowed going on to explain what she dislikes most is the name: "I mean *cheese* doesn't belong in a cake. Cake should be chocolatey or at least sweet like... oh look! they have apple crumble. I love that!"

"Judith have you ever eaten cheesecake?" he demands.

Giving him a puzzled look she replies: "No, of course not. I told you, just the name puts me off."

He's about to remonstrate when both of his sisters burst into peals of laughter then completely shut him out while they tell Judith about themselves and their families, and ask her plenty of questions, too.

Normally the introverted woman would be overwhelmed but she can feel their friendly caring and is surprisingly comfortable in their company. Grant resigns himself to simply enjoying his decadent dessert.

Judith is fascinated looking from one twin to the other. Grant's sisters are only the second set of twins she's ever met in her life, and the only adults. The women are distinguishable because of different make-up and hairstyles but each glance shows how they've aged in a similar fashion.

Addy, the eldest by six minutes, has coloured her chin-length blonde hair with tawny lowlights, while a natural gray blends into Abby's blonde waves.

Both sisters are exuberant and animated finishing each other's sentences and exclaiming with shock and delight as they relate family stories. They often exchange looks in silent communication and will suddenly burst out laughing over a shared thought.

Grant had already told Judith that he had a big family with lots of nieces and nephews. Addy explains that she has three boys and one girl and Abby has three girls and two boys but adds that: "They're identical twins as well so they kind of count as one. It's always that way with twins, they become a unit of *the twins* rather than two boys."

"We know that from firsthand experience ourselves," puts in Abby, before continuing: "How many brothers and sisters do you have?"

Judith feels slightly lacking as she answers: "Oh, I'm an only child."

Addy and Abby respond with wide-eyes and mouths in O-shapes saying *you lucky thing!*

Judith laughs happily stating: "Hey, that saying about *the grass is always greener*... is true!"

"I hate to break up this giggle-fest," interrupts Grant, "but we've got to finish up if I'm going to make it into work on time."

The three women glance at phones and watches exclaiming over the fact that over two hours has passed by. Grant settles the bill with a huff of annoyance when he's told that cash isn't allowed and then hurries them through their goodbyes.

As soon as they get in the car to drive home Grant kisses Judith who then enthuses over meeting Addy and Abby.

"They're so nice! and you never told me your sisters were twins, do twins run in your family? They said you were spoiled rotten as a kid. Their kids sound great, you must have a lot of fun at Christmas–"

Grant interrupts all her questions stating: "Well I certainly have a lot of expenses at Christmas," But he's laughing as he says it.

As a rule Judith keeps her emotions firmly buttoned down so he loves seeing this excited and happy side to her. He knew his sisters would love her as will their families. He finds himself looking forward to the holidays for the first time in a long time, in fact not since his mother passed away. He and Judith will definitely be part of this year's Christmas celebration even if it is via Zoom.

"So tell me the truth, were your sisters teasing me or did you really used to sneak their bubble-bath?"

"It was once!" he exclaims full of righteous resentment as Judith gasps out a stuttering laugh. "First of all, I was like eight years old at the time, and secondly we ran out of *Mr. Bubble*," Grant is indignant as Judith collapses in a fit of giggles. She completely loses herself in hysterical mirth when he goes on to explain: "I had no idea that their stuff would stink so strongly of lavender that the whole house would know I used it."

Grant finds the joy of Judith's laughter contagious and ends up joining in. "Stop!" she pants, "My cheeks hurt!"

"Oh yeah? Well, my stomach hurts," he retorts and exploding into a new round of laughter she answers: "That's what you get for eating cake made out of cheese!"

Grant just shakes his head smiling. "Oh I can argue with you over that but I've got to get going so hold that thought." He leans in for a kiss and after a moment enjoying each other's lips he murmurs: "I'm so glad you had a good time with my sisters."

"I really did, Grant. Now I feel silly for trying to put off the meeting. They're both great!"

Judith exits the car and Grant waits until she's got the lobby door open before waving and driving off. When Judith gets to her apartment she opens the door to darkness. Flipping the hall switch to light her way she heads into the living-room illuminated only by the twinkling bulbs on the Christmas tree.

Beth sits on the couch and beside her is the same young man Judith saw at the convenience store. Immediately reaching to turn on the table lamp Judith stares dumbly at the pair, unsure how to react.

Beth is perfectly relaxed as she greets: "Oh hello, Judith. Is it late? it's gotten awfully dark. Oh, this is my friend Dusty, er... Dustin actually, Dustin Matthews."

The young man stands extending his hand to Judith and wearing a charming, lopsided smile claims: "This is a pleasure Principal Taylor, I've heard a lot about you."

Upon hearing her title Judith gathers her wits and assumes the role bestowed by her job. Standing tall she gives Dusty's hand a brisk shake before looking pointedly at the couch the two have been sitting on. Beth is the picture of innocence but the boy colours up realizing how things must look. His confidence falters and he remains silent.

Beth's artless comment about Judith's beautiful Tiffany lamp leaves the older woman studying the girl closely. Beth's hair isn't mussed and her lips aren't swollen so it looks like Judith didn't interrupt a kissing session. Her shoulders slump in relief. She can't imagine that Brian Penner would be very happy to think Judith had aided his daughter in a clandestine *tryst*.

It honestly does seem like the two were so wrapped up in their conversation they didn't notice the shadows overtaking the room.

A high-pitched mew draws everyone's attention to the kitten who jumps off the couch to trot over to Judith. Before the cat can snag her stockings Judith scoops up Panda and kisses her nose.

"How was my girl? Were you a good kitty? Did you miss me?" The tension has broken with the nonsense talk and Dusty, still standing, tells Beth he should get going and is she ready to leave?

"Oh I'll drive you, both of you," Judith says but Beth shakes her head saying: "No need, Dusty can drive me."

Foolishly Judith blurts out: "In a car?"

The two youngsters give her an odd look before Beth confirms that *yes, Dusty has a car, a Range Rover*. Judith doesn't know a lot about cars but she's pretty sure that's an expensive vehicle. Her expression has settled into a frown and the boy is quick to assure her that he's a careful driver and will see that Beth gets home safely.

With that the two of them leave and Judith, locking the door behind them, returns to the living-room absentmindedly agreeing with Beth's admiration of how pretty her table lamp looks with it's colours glowing brightly. Panda's purrs attract her attention and she takes the kitten into the kitchen for a meal.

"What on earth am I going to say to Lila?" she wonders.

Judith Tattles

Lila answers her phone with a cheery "Hi Judith, what's up?"

"We have to talk and I don't even know where to start."

"Uh-oh, that sounds ominous," replies Lila but Judith can hear the teasing in her voice.

"Well it is but not for me for you. Well... maybe for you but most likely Beth..."

"Beth? What do you mean?"

Loudly exhaling Judith begins: "Well... it's kind of awkward because you know how I hate to get involved in people's personal business, I mean it's always so messy, but Grant says I have to do the right thing and well, you're my friend and I like Beth... but I had no idea he'd come over to the apartment although I'm absolutely certain nothing happened but dammit I feel like a tattletale–"

Lila cuts in asking: "Is this about Dusty?"

"Oh! Oh, you already know about him? Oh thank goodness!"

"I do. Beth told me everything including inviting him over to your place which I told her was totally out of line without your permission. She said she knew you wouldn't mind and I explained she couldn't possibly know any such thing and then she said– forget that! the point is I'm on her side but we haven't figured out how to broach the subject with Brian yet."

"You're okay with this boy seeing Beth?"

"Sure. Young love and all that. I think it's sweet."

"But have you met him? Have you even seen him?"

"No I haven't, but Beth took a selfie of the two of them on her phone and he's a cutie."

"Lila, I'm pretty sure he has a tattoo on his neck!"

"He does! It's an owl which Beth tells me represents wisdom and spiritual growth. Of course any tattoo represents rebellion against his parents but I didn't tell her that."

"Well duh, I guess. Assuming his parents are even around and care about what he's getting up to, that is."

"Judith! What are you talking about?"

"Well this fellow, this Dusty, is he really the kind of boy you'd like Beth to associate with?"

"Dusty? Why would you... oh I get it! Judith, you called to warn me! that's so sweet. Listen, Dusty is dressing up like a bad boy to punish his father. His family are cattle ranchers, piles of money, but his parents are talking divorce because Dad got caught with another woman. From what Dusty told Beth it was a one-night stand, not a girlfriend or mistress, and the father is repentant so it sounds like the parents will figure it out okay on their own. Meanwhile Dusty is overreacting. Well, we both know what the young are like.

So although he's dressing up and acting up, got a tattoo and got his ear pierced, he's definitely from a good home and is just being an angry kid right now. He even got a late-night part-time job that's totally messing with his school attendance and that got him kicked off the football team. His father must be furious about that. Anyhow, I'm hoping Beth can help get Dusty back on track."

"Oh Lila I can't tell you what a relief it is to hear this. I was totally thinking *juvenile delinquent* and that Brian would blame me for I don't know, encouraging them? anyhow phew. I mean, what if they had had sex? what if he got her pregnant? what if he got her a tattoo?!!"

Lila can't hold back her laughter at the shocked outrage in Judith's voice.

"Don't laugh at me! I really was agonizing over telling you. Then I remembered how everyone got mad at me for keeping quiet when I witnessed that argument between Holly and that Billy MacNeill, and then Grant basically told me I had to tell you so I'm really glad you already knew. I guess it's a good sign that Beth told you."

"It is. She really is a nice girl and didn't like the idea of sneaking around as if they were doing something underhanded. She isn't sure how to approach her father, but she wanted someone to know."

"And it's great that she's comfortable coming to you with something like this. She respects and trust you, Lila."

"Yeah, and that feels really good."

"So I guess I was right in thinking he drives an expensive car?"

"For sure! His Range Rover would have cost about four or five times as much as your Subaru, and you've got a nice car."

"Of course coming from money doesn't automatically mean he's got to be a good guy."

"True, but they haven't even kissed yet so I think he is a decent kid. I'm glad Beth has met someone even if it's doubtful that they'll develop a relationship since they're both so young. But I'm sure she's been feeling a bit left out of things now that her Dad and I are officially dating and it's more than just friendship between us. We three get along great and enjoy being together, but it's only natural she'd prefer to find a friend of her own.

So I'm happy for her but now, the real problem is: how do we break the news to Brian?"

Noel Larkin's Annual Party

Grant, Lila, and Brian all travel to the Frampton residence in Judith's car since she's their designated driver. Brian remarked that Detective Grant couldn't very well get picked up on an impaired charge at a Police *Spot Check* being the boss and all. "Unless they'd give you a pass?" he asks.

"We don't have the R.I.D.E. programme here in Edgemont," Grant replies mildly but he's slightly annoyed at Brian's assumption. "But if I was stopped and failed the roadside test then yes, I would be charged and breathalyzed. The consequences for me would be very bad but for you, Brian? they'd be disastrous to your business if you couldn't drive."

"God yeah, you've got that right," agrees Brian. Completely unaware of the barb in Grant's tone he leans forward in his seat to thank Judith for taking care of them.

Brian's honest appreciation soothes Grant's irritation. With a deprecatory chuckle he asks: "Why do I let your needling of me about my profession bug me so much? There's nothing funny about being a policeman."

"Oh it's not the job Grant, it's you. You look like you should be on the cover of one of those romance novels Beth reads instead of wearing a cop uniform. I realize you don't wear one now but you used to, right?"

Before Grant can reply Judith interrupts indignantly asking: "Beth reads trashy romance?"

"No one said *trashy,* but yeah she enjoys romances. Why not? What would you call *Wuthering Heights* or *Pride and Prejudice?*"

"Well I'd call them *classics* but... I suppose you're right. They would have been merely romances in their day."

"In other words, women have always read romance novels and will continue to do so. Mushy, hearts-and-flowers romanticism that reality can never live up to, it's so stupid."

"Believe me Brian, no man can live up to the men in today's romances and I'm not talking about their hearts," quips Lila.

He scoffs before stopping to say: "Wait a minute, Beth reads this stuff?"

"You don't, do you Judith?" asks Grant.

Judith looks in the rearview mirror to meet Lila's gaze and is rewarded by her friend rolling her eyes at the men.

The mansion has been professionally decorated for the season and is all lit up with hundreds of white bulbs and silver icicle ornaments.

"It's like a fairy-tale palace," exclaims Judith in wonder.

Lila echoes the sentiment saying: "It's magical." She's more bubbly than usual tonight and her exuberance has her bouncing in her seat, ready to *party hard*.

Judith parks on the road. Despite the cold weather it's been a dry winter and they can walk easily on pavement that's free of snow. As they get out of the car Lila instructs Judith, who is a few inches taller, to bend down. When she does Lila shakes some sparkles over the top of Judith's hair.

"What are you doing!"

"I'm making you festive!" declares Lila.

Outraged Judith practically shouts "I already am festive!"

"Well then festiver," an unrepentant Lila smirks.

Distracted, Judith stops trying to brush the glitter from her hair to say: "*Festiver* is not a word."

"I said it so it must be!" giggles Lila triumphantly.

Judith just stares at her friend who is behaving in such a peculiar manner. "Lila, are you drunk?"

"Not in the least little bit," Lila claims, twirling her way towards the Frampton residence. "I'm just in a wonderful *festiver* mood!"

Her carefree joy is infectious and stops Judith from complaining further. Especially when she turns to Grant to take his arm only to notice how intently he's staring at her. He sees the pretty colours shining in her hair and her face, particularly her eyes, wearing make-up for the party and he drinks in her beauty murmuring: "Judith, I love you."

Startled by this public display of affection from the usually reserved man Judith's eyes widen and her mouth forms an O-shape. Grant can't resist and leans in for a kiss, surprising Judith even more.

"See Judith? Those sparkles have Christmas magic," shouts Lila as she skips and dances, pulling Brian along with her.

The lights cover both sides of the walkway leading to the front door which holds a huge spruce wreath adorned with frothy white lace and satin ribbons. They're welcomed indoors by a middle-aged woman, either a housekeeper or an employee of the catering firm, who takes their outdoor things and directs them to go through into the house.

Noel greets the foursome with enthusiasm, kissing Judith and Lila and shaking the men's hands. Lila hands him the birthday card they've all signed that includes a thank-you from the charity to whom they've donated a cash gift in his name.

Noel and Annabelle got married in the summer and they make a handsome, happy couple. They continue to live here in the home of his Aunt Eleanor, a warm gracious woman. Also a very wealthy woman and Noel doesn't need to work but he's a gifted teacher who enjoys his job. Both Judith and Lila consider him a good friend, although Annabelle is still somewhat of a stranger to them.

"This is such fun," Noel confides, "We have to shuffle people in and out in groups because of the limit on numbers, so if I suddenly holler *everybody out of the pool* you'll know you're getting the boot!" he laughs, his eyes bright with excitement.

"So get your drinks in quickly," stage-whispers Annabelle, as equally delighted as her husband, shooing them towards the buffet tables arranged against one wall. The food looks delicious and the staff are attentive.

Everything is presented perfectly and the partygoers fills their plates choosing from a sumptuous selection. After confirming it's non-alcoholic Judith ladles a cup of punch for herself while the others head to the bar.

"Ginger ale for me, please," requests Lila.

"Oh you're the designated driver tonight so Brian can get pissed?" teases Noel.

"No, that's my job. To be the designated driver, I mean, not to get pissed! I'm driving the three of them," answers Judith joining the group. Noel orders the bartender to serve up the best whiskey to the men and the three of them move to the side.

Turning to her friend Judith says: "Lila, if you don't feel like a drink-drink yet why not join me in this punch? It's delicious!"

Eleanor overhears this comment and replies: "I'm glad you like it, Judith. It's from an old family recipe."

"Ah, a jealousy guarded secret?"

"Of course! but since you're one of my favourite people I could be persuaded to share it with you under a strict vow of silence, of course," says the older woman with a wink.

"That's so nice of you, Eleanor. It's hard to find a festive punch-without-a-punch that don't taste like *Kool-Aid*."

After promising to have cook write out the recipe Eleanor turns to mingle with her other guests while Judith gets a firm hold on Lila's arm and dragging her off to a corner commands: "Spill."

"What? What are you talking about?" huffs Lila but she can't hide a smirk struggling to get free.

"Ginger ale? when there's all this lovely booze and hot toddies and rum-soaked eggnog and spiced cider? Ginger ale is for upset tummies but you're too over-the-top excited tonight to be sick so that means...?"

Lila clutches her friends arm hissing: "Judith, I can't say anything to you. I have to tell Brian first—"

"Omigod you ARE!!!"

Laughing with joy Lila confirms: "Yes, I *are*. But you can't breathe a word, seriously, I haven't told Brian yet."

"He'll be thrilled."

Nodding with enthusiasm Lila agrees: "Yes, he will. It's a perfect Christmas present, even better than a cat!"

"Ha! Okay, yes I'll concede that Brian would rather have a baby than a kitten. God knows why..." she jokes.

Assuming a thoughtful expression Lila says: "Beth will be over the moon at this news but it will also push her a little further away from us and closer to Dusty. I just hope he doesn't break her heart."

"Absolutely. But it's okay if she breaks his, right?"

"Well it's not ideal but a break-up at some future date is inevitable and selfishly I want him to have the heartache, not her."

Their conversation is interrupted by a sudden influx of guests and in their unofficial roles as civic leaders the Larkins and Eleanor Frampton uphold the rules and start saying goodbye and Merry Christmas to the earlier wave of guests.

"Oh I'm sure you four don't have to go yet," says Annabelle revelling at being the centre of attention from three very handsome men. She's obviously forgiven Grant for taking her to the police station to be questioned last year. He disagreed with that decision, and having it forced on him to enact when everyone knew it was a political move.

Now he says: "Well I'm a cop so I kinda *have to* follow the rules, and as for Principal Taylor over there well... I think *setting a good example* is part of her job description." He smiles down at the pretty newlywed who pouts but snuggles up to her husband.

"Happy Birthday, Noel," says Judith, giving him a quick hug.

"Thanks Principal Judith and that reminds me, I want to talk to you but obviously not now, but can I call you in a couple of days?"

"Of course but can't you give me a hint what this is about? otherwise it will prey on my mind."

"Oh sure! It's about the school play or rather the school play that wasn't."

Annabelle has been listening to the conversation and she now puts in her two-cent's worth saying: "That's two years in a row there was no school play at Edgemont Girls' School in December. It's really not fair on Noel, he loves doing the play."

Judith is well aware that the annual play had to be cancelled twice due to reasons completely beyond the school's control but she can tell Annabelle is a little tipsy so she let's the criticism pass. She turns her attention back to Noel who explains that he'd like to do an end-of-school-year play this coming year.

"Instead of the December play?"

"I was thinking in addition to... what do you think?"

"I think it sounds like a lot of extra work but if you're willing then yes, of course. The play has been sorely missed and doing two plays in 2021 will raise everyone's spirits."

"Judith I'm so glad you're the principal!" he practically shouts, drawing the amused attention of the people around them.

She gravely accepts his compliment but then smiles and says she's sure Pat Johnson would have agreed as well.

Lila joins them then saying: "A very Merry Christmas to both of you, your first Christmas as a married couple!" Both Annabelle and Noel beam and give back their own *Merry Christmas* wishes before welcoming a large party who've just arrived.

The foursome's coats are retrieved and within minutes they are bundled up and then bundled out the door. The house hadn't felt too warm but the coolness of the night air is welcome.

"It's too early to call it a night so come back to my place," says Judith. "I'll still drive you back to your home after."

"Oh thanks Judith but actually we planned on continuing the party at Brian's. The food is already there waiting and most of it's courtesy of Mrs Piernitsky which means it's good and there's plenty of it."

"Sounds perfect!" chimes in Grant.

"But Beth's at my place looking after Panda–"

"Oh right! Well we'll swing by your apartment and grab Beth on the way home. I'm sure the kitty can take care of herself for a few hours."

Judith casts a helpless look at Grant who thinks she's overreacting before narrowing his eyes in understanding. Beth must have Dusty visiting and Judith is hoping to leave the decision-making on that budding relationship up to Brian with some input from Lila, no doubt. Grant isn't pleased, he thinks everything should be out in the open and if Brian says *no dating* then that's that.

"I'll text my girl a heads-up now, and then I'll let her know when we arrive." Despite the huge size of Brian's hands his fingers fly over his mobile. The chime signalling a new message comes in shortly after. Judith discovers she's holding her breath as Brian reads aloud: "Sounds great, we'll meet you downstairs."

"I guess she had a friend come by, I hope she asked your permission first, Judith?"

"Oh! um... Yeah I think I remember something–" A new chime saves her from getting even more muddled.

Brian asks: "Is it okay to just push the lock on the door handle? That must be for you, Judith."

"Mmm, yes. Tell her *yes that will be fine.*" She turns her attention back to the road but sneaking a glance in the mirror at Lila sees that her friend's eyes are sparkling with mirth. Judith doesn't like to be distracted when driving so Grant doesn't try to take her hand but he does rest his own on her thigh. She's comforted by its warmth but grows increasingly anxious as they draw closer to her apartment.

Sure enough Beth and Dusty and standing in the vestibule, coming through the front door when they spot Judith's headlights and joining the adults in the car.

Brian's large drink of good quality Scotch must have mellowed him because he reins in his surprise at seeing his daughter with a young man only saying: "And who is this, Beth?"

"My friend Dusty, Dusty Matthews."

The young man politely shakes hands as Beth continues to introduce him to everyone. Lila gushes a bit while Grant simply nods in acknowledgement.

"We won't all fit in my car!" Judith blurts out.

"Oh that's not a problem Ms. Taylor. I have to go to work so I have my own ride."

"Well I hope we'll see you again soon, Dusty," says Lila drawing Brian back into Judith's car. Grant opens Judith's door and she slips in behind the wheel, watching Beth and Dusty from the corner of her eye.

Grant doesn't look at the youngsters as he walks around the front of the car to the passenger side, but he does notice Brian's eyes are glued to his daughter. They can't hear what the teenagers are saying but they do hear Beth's happy laugh as she shoves Dusty in the chest before turning to get into the backseat beside Lila.

Judith's shoulders slump in relief, and Lila whispers in Brian's ear that she has a lovely surprise waiting for him at home.

The End of 2020

Lila has met up with Judith at Edgemont School for Girls in the week between Christmas and New Year's to help take down the artificial Christmas tree from the foyer and remove the red-and-green construction paper chains that decorate the hallways.

"You do realize that Mr. Glover will make a bit of a fuss saying that this clean-up is his job and since he's the custodian he'll be right."

"Oh I know but I'll only worry if he starts climbing ladders at his age. Of course I can't tell him that so I'll just say that as single women we found the time heavy on our hands. That's something he'll believe. No doubt Mrs. Glover is near worn-out from all the Christmas preparation. I'm sure she does all the shopping, wrapping, decorating, baking, cooking, and cleaning in their house."

"I bet you're right but I'd also bet on him doing all the snow shovelling, taking the garbage out, and looking after getting their car winterized."

"Hmm, yes. An elderly couple sticking to their traditional roles and perfectly happy to do so." The two women, both in recently formed relationships, muse about family life. They each had a very enjoyable Christmas holiday.

Lila breaks the spell first saying: "We're gearing up to get ready for the grand re-opening of The Centre in February so we'll need your expertise with the books again Judith, if you'll have time?"

"Yes, being principal feels more like taking on a role rather than doing a job. Turns out I'm Principal Taylor 24/7, I don't get to switch off at the end of the work day, but I'm okay with that. Pat was right when she said I'd learn a lot about myself once I stepped out of my safety zone.

So, back on topic yes I will certainly get the books set up for The Centre. Actually, I just had an idea... we could add a course of learning the accounting software to the senior girls curriculum and use The Centre as a teaching model. I'll ask Samira to look into getting an educational licence for the programme."

"That's a great idea, Judith. Knowing basic bookkeeping is a necessary life-skill and proficiency in any software is handy on a resume."

"Let's see, classes are scheduled starting January 11 so we'll be able to dive right in. Of course some details will have to be mocked up – can't have the girls gossiping about so-and-so always being in arrears with their membership dues – but I'll come up with a workaround for that. February will be here before we know it."

"I'm really glad about opening up again because the kids need the outlet of organized sports and plenty of people have already put their names down for different fitness classes. But it's kind of bitter-sweet since February 8 is the one-year anniversary of Rev Robbie's death. It's going to be a hard time for a lot of people. He touched so many lives and always in a positive way."

"Then turn it into a celebration of all the wonderful things he did for people, and the wonderful man he that he was. I'm sure his funeral brought closure to many but Lila for people like you who automatically connect February with his murder well... why not do something special? Instead of *pretending and moving on* do something to help everyone acknowledge the bad memories and replace them with fellowship?"

Lila's eyes glisten with emotion that she tries to hide by poking her friend in the arm and saying: "You're a wise woman Principal Taylor."

* * *

Reg knows that Jerry Bennett, the manager of the trailer park, doesn't miss much and will have seen his car pull up.

I'm sure he knows why I'm here, thinks Reg as he walks up the newly cleared path to the man's door. He knocks and waits, knowing it's late but he can see the glow of a TV shining through the curtains. The outside light comes on and after a moment Jerry opens the door.

"Detective Osborne, what brings you out here at this time of night? No trouble, I hope?"

Reg recognizes a bluff when he hears one and he simply chuckles before saying: "Put on a warm coat, Jerry, we've got a job to do."

"What, now? What do you mean?" but the manager is already stepping into his boots and slipping on his jacket. It's a well-worn Hudson's Bay blanket coat that Reg both admires and envies for its comfort and warmth.

"Those Christmas decorations on your green space need to come down and be returned to their rightful owners."

"Are you accusing me of theft?"

"Nope, in fact I'm quite sure you aren't the culprit."

"Well then you're saying I've got stolen goods on the property and that's just as bad. I'll have you know–"

Reg hurries the man along telling him: "I'm not accusing and I'm not investigating. We're simply going to remove the evidence. Now c'mon, it's cold and it's late and we've got work to do."

Jerry just shakes his head, but he stops arguing and goes along with Reg.

The two men arrive at the common area and pause for a moment to enjoy the spectacle. There's more than a dozen colourful inflatables, some of them lit from within powered by a solar panel. They quickly deflate the decorations and roll up the plastic. At one point someone calls out *what's going on over there?* but Jerry reassures them and realizing it's the trailer park manager the person retreats.

Looking at the sizable pile Reg states: "We're gonna need your pick-up to haul this stuff out of here." Jerry agrees telling Reg to stay put and he'll be right back. The night has turned cold and Reg stamps his feet to keep them warm but Jerry doesn't keep him waiting long. The truck arrives and they toss the decorations in the back.

"Follow me to that Tim Horton's near the police station. We'll toss these in the dumpster but we'll leave a couple of pieces lying out in the parking lot so the cops can't miss it when they get their morning coffee. The patrolmen will be heroes for solving the case, the crime will be vandalism born out of envy, and the owners can get their property back if they haven't already collected on the insurance."

"Would they bother to submit a claim?"

"Of course! that's how the rich stay rich. Besides, the cheapest of these inflatables is over $100 and look how many pieces there are. Jerry you're not a stupid man. You must have seen these things for sale at Canadian Tire and you know nobody in this trailer park would shell out that kind of money for Christmas decorations.

You turned a blind eye to the thefts but... I'm sure these kids got the thrill of a lifetime and all the residents would have enjoyed the display too so your heart was in the right place.

Just don't do it again next year! Detective Grant is going crazy filling out the reports."

"Fair enough, but tell me Detective Osborne–"

"Call me Reg since we're partners-in-crime now."

"Okay thanks Reg. Tell me what made you decide to *aid and abet* me? "

"Oh that's easy - tthis year I wanted Edgemont to have a crimeless Christmas."

Epilogue

Grant has to work New Year's Eve but he manages to swing by Judith's place before midnight to celebrate the end of 2020. He brings a half-bottle of non-alcoholic champagne, a small chocolate cheesecake that he simply calls a *torte* in order to get Judith to share it with him, a bag of cat treats for Panda, and a stunning princess-cut diamond engagement ring.

Judith is shocked. She was surprised at her disappointment when there was no ring box under the tree at Christmas. Surprised, because she'd been retreating when she felt Grant pushing and rushing her. She should have been relieved, but instead had to swallow an unexpected feeling of being let down.

Lila vocalized plenty of disillusionment and dismay on Judith's behalf. She didn't get a ring either but since Brian is *over the moon* at the baby news a wedding is being planned *asap!*

Staring at the what she considers the most beautiful, the most perfect ring she's ever seen, Judith is at a loss for words. When Grant prompts her for a response she says: "But I thought... er, when nothing happened at Christmas... um, well I just figured you didn't... you know."

Puzzled by her stuttering reaction Grant hurries to explain: "My sisters said *don't make the ring just another Christmas present, make the proposal a special occasion all by itself.* Oh Judith, I hate that you thought that I... oh sweetheart, I love you so much and I want to marry you."

Judith answers by flinging her arms around Grant's neck and giving him a kiss that carries them right into 2021.

Preview the Series!

First book in the Village of Edgemont Cozy Mysteries series

A Deadly December
in Edgemont

Della North

Chapter One

The body of missing teen Holly Lezinsky was found on December 19th, just two days before her fourteenth birthday. She'd been missing for one week and pregnant for eleven.

The discovery didn't affect Judith's plans for Christmas because she didn't have any, but she did have to rearrange the school's ruined holiday schedule. "Luckily there are only a few more days left, and the workload is light," she thought.

Although the news was sad Judith felt it was important that they learned the truth at last. It had been a very unsettling week for staff and students alike as everyone worried over Holly's whereabouts. She was a popular girl.

School Principal Patricia Johnson got the call from the police. They would be coming around later today or tomorrow with questions and to hold some interviews because it was a suspicious death. Well of course it was, the victim was just a child although Judith was quite sure Holly didn't see herself as such!

Pat answered the officer's call herself since Samira, the school secretary, was off sick with the flu. A nasty bug making the rounds had already affected staff and students. She called Judith and apologised for giving her the news over the phone but excused that claiming a pounding headache and a million things to do adding:

"I'll have to make an announcement but I'm hoping to get more information from the police first. Everyone's going to have so many questions. Ugh, I just can't think about it all right now."

Judith discovered that she wasn't shocked to hear the new, figuring she must have suspected that Holly was already dead. Holly did seem like the kind of girl to get into trouble. Unless it was suicide? How was she killed? Unfortunately, it wasn't a stretch to imagine Holly as a murder victim.

Judith did wonder "Am I being unfair to the girl?" but then an image of Holly in her school uniform came to mind: plaid skirt rolled up at the waist to shorten it, shirt unbuttoned to show the lace on her bra, and knee socks rolled down to her ankles to flash a lot of bare leg.

Holly Lezinsky was a brazen adolescent flaunting her new-found sexuality but the poor girl didn't deserve to die.

Of course, Judith felt terribly sorry for the girl's family. Holly was raised by a single mom and she was an only child, an upbringing similar to Judith's own. She started wondering about how her own mother would have coped in such a circumstance but forcefully slammed the door shut on such thoughts. The past was dead and gone. She had resolved a long time ago to move on.

Still, it seemed that somehow a death was made even worse when it happened so close to Christmas. Judith thought that the happiness of others would be unbearable to the bereaved. And then each successive anniversary would be another reminder.

"Well, it's not my concern. It's up to the police now," thought Judith. Opening the scheduling app on her laptop she forgot about the girl and got to work revising the plans for the next few days.

Chapter Two

She got back to work thinking "No more distractions, I definitely want to finish the Accounts Receivable today. I'm not going to let this delay me starting my holidays tomorrow," Judith decided. "I suppose that's selfish but honestly this girl's death is nothing to do with me."

Her phone buzzed with another internal call from the principal. Judith sighed. Pat Johnson came straight to the point saying:

"Judith, I hope you haven't booked anything because I can't let you go on vacation yet. I need you here. I could have managed on my own without my secretary but not with Holly's death as well. The phone is ringing non-stop. In fact, I need you to come to my office now, can you do that?"

Frustrated, Judith banged down the handset. She definitely did not want to act as School Secretary for the day but she felt she owed Pat. So, she had no choice, she had to go to the principal right away.

"But I will stand up for my rights," Judith asserted. "I'm determined to fight for my holiday time!" She smoothed her hair back from her face, it was brown like her eyes, and tended to frizz if not kept under control. Judith usually didn't much bother about her appearance – so long as she was clean and tidy – but right now it was important not to look frazzled. She wanted to present a calm but determined demeanor. Hurrying to the suite at the end of the corridor she planned her arguments along the way.

The moment she arrived in the principal's office Judith realized her time off was going to be cancelled for sure. It was obvious that Pat was sick, her face damp with the sheen of fever and her eyes dull. Judith was torn between sympathy for Pat's plight and her own self-pity. She resigned herself to hear disappointing news.

Lila Morelli, the school's nurse, entered the room a few moments later saying:

"You've caught the flu, Principal Johnson. And on top of the tragic news about poor Holly Lezinski, too. Your resistance will be really low."

Judith had met the new hire earlier in the month. As school bursar it was her job to put together Ms. Morelli's employment orientation package of passcodes, tax forms, and benefits. Afterwards Lila lingered but Judith had no interest in small talk or coworker gossip and hurried her on her way. Seeing Lila in professional mode was interesting.

"Professional except for the hair, that is." Judith amended, eyeing the turquoise streaks in Lila's blonde pageboy.

Nurse Morelli wore a white medical jacket over regular clothes, not scrubs or a uniform. She pulled a digital thermometer out of her pocket and checked the older woman's temperature at wrist and then at forehead.

"Normal temp, no fever," she announced.

Judith perked up at the happy news, saying:

"Great, not flu then."

But Lila shook her head answering:

"No, that doesn't mean no flu it simply means the virus can thrive instead of breaking with a high temperature. When the fever hits, and it almost definitely will, you'll be better off in bed. Principal Johnson is there anyone at home, or who could come to your home, to keep an eye on you?"

"Oh yes, yes really, I'm okay. There's no need to fuss. My husband took early retirement to pursue his hobbies from home. He'll look after me."

She struggled to get up and both women hurried to give assistance. Frail and shaky – this was not the Patricia Johnson Judith was used to seeing!

"Judith, you'll follow the usual procedure and step in for me?" Pat pleaded.

Judith struggled to keep her thoughts from showing on her face. She hadn't want to take over the secretary's job and now it looked like she was getting the added burden of the principal's duties. She wanted to take her vacation break! However...

"Of course, Pat. Don't worry about a thing, just concentrate on getting better. We'll be fine," she soothed.

Turning to Lila Morelli she added:

"Well, Nurse Morelli, I'm afraid you'll have to help me while both Samira and Principal Johnson are absent." Judith resented sounding petulant. She spotted Lila Morelli's poorly disguised smirk and was surprised to find herself smiling back.

"Well, Bursar Taylor, since we've been thrown together, I suggest you call me Lila. Sound good, Judith?"

Chapter Three

Judith was busy studying the more extensive calendar, filled with appointments and class schedules, in the principal's office when Lila returned from helping Patricia Johnson into her car.

The principal had insisted on driving it home since she and her husband only had the one vehicle. Lila tried to organize one teacher to drive and another to follow in their own car, but Pat resisted getting anyone else involved. Judith had listened to the exchange without comment, she knew Pat was stubborn so there was no point arguing.

"Principal Johnson has given us a dozen things to do, most of which won't get done, but she had one very good suggestion," said Lila. "We can direct all the incoming phone calls to the staff room phone. That way everything will get picked up by the answering machine. She explained how it's done and it's a simple redirect."

"Yes of course, I forgot about that. It's something Samira does but not often."

Judith told Lila how the protocol had been established years before and was carried out whenever the admin office was unable to answer calls.

"Since the staff can't be expected to take down messages – some of which are quite lengthy! – while enjoying their well-deserved break every caller is asked to leave their information.

If someone in the break-room is expecting a call they are able to pick up the handset and have their conversation. The only drawback to the system is that anyone and everyone can hear the messages. People have warned friends and family about this and to be discreet, but people forget, and some calls are definitely amusing!"

"It sounds like a good idea and something we can definitely use for the rest of the semester."

"I think we're going to have to cancel classes and start the holidays a day or so early," said Judith. "So many staff and students are off sick. And now, with the news of Holly's death, I don't think the students will be able to concentrate. I'm sure even the teachers will be gossiping about it."

"Well, from what I remember of my school days not a lot got done in the time before Christmas anyhow."

"No, there are no exams or anything. The younger children make Christmas cards and chains out of construction paper. The middle group read Christmas stories, and the older girls are busy preparing for the play. Oh no, Holly had a starring role in the play!"

"This is my first Christmas here, so I don't know how important the play is--"

"It matters," interrupted Judith, "but with this flu bug going 'round we'll have to cancel the performance. Some of the cast are sick already and to sit in a closed room with a bunch of people who are sniffling, sneezing, and coughing... ugh! It will have to be rescheduled for some time in the New Year. Can't be helped."

"What play are they doing?"

"Their own. Noel Larkin – have you met him yet? – he's the Drama teacher and he gets them to write a script, play the parts, make costumes and scenery, everything in fact. It always has some sort of a Christmas theme. The parents love it."

"I do know Noel, he's invited me to his Christmas party, along with the rest of the staff, that is."

"Yes, it's a combination birthday and Christmas event. He was actually born on the 25th hence the name choice."

"I like the name Noel, it's unusual. And he seems like a nice guy, in fact considering how good-looking he is he's surprisingly nice."

"Hmm, never thought of him that way but you're right he is a nice man."

"And handsome too, remember," said Lila with a smile and a question in her voice. Judith wasn't paying attention; she was too busy studying the big calendar. She self-described as 'detail-oriented' and was reading every entry. She replied offhandedly:

"If you like the 'male model' type, then sure."

"Ha, that does fit him. So do you prefer the rugged he-man type?" Lila teased.

"I don't have a type," Judith retorted.

"'Okay Lila don't go there', I get it."

Judith rolled her eyes, saying: "I'm just not interested."

"So, is the party a fun thing? or does it feel like a work outing?"

"I don't know, I've never gone."

"Oh, sorry, I thought everyone was invited."

"Well of course I'm always invited, yes, but I don't mix with my coworkers as a rule."

Lila answered using a pretend-whiny tone: "Does that mean you won't go with me to show me the ropes, as it were?"

"I wouldn't know the 'ropes' if I tripped over them." Judith caught herself smiling, enjoying this unaccustomed banter. She found that she couldn't help but like Lila.

"Besides, when it comes to socializing with coworkers, I think you'll find the teachers consider themselves a cut above the rest of the staff. They seem friendly but they aren't exactly welcoming," Judith said with a shrug, "Maybe things will be different for you."

Lila sidestepped that comment by asking: "So how do we go about cancelling the rest of the school year?"

"We'll get everyone into the auditorium and make an announcement—-"

"Yes, Principal Johnson wanted us to tell the girls about Holly and have a minute's silence. We can combine that with notice about the school closure."

"Well, that's the other thing. Many of the parents are at work during the day so we have to give them some notice before sending the girls home. The best thing to do is have the school open for the next couple of days, but attendance can be optional. For the students, that is, the teachers will still have to come in. Then, depending on how many students show up, we can decide to stay open or close.

For sure we'll close on the 24th. Usually, we're open for a half-day of snacks and socializing, card and gift exchanges, and then the school play takes place in the afternoon. This year we'll just have to tell everyone to stay home. I don't think even a small party would be appropriate."

"Oh, do you think Noel will cancel his party?"

"No, and nobody would expect him to do so. But it's different for the school. Holly was one of us and the parents expect us to observe the proprieties."

"You're in charge, Judith, so get on the PA system and call everyone to the assembly. I'll go organize the chairs into rows."

With Lila gone Judith took a moment to gear herself up. The announcement was no problem, she could easily speak into the microphone, but standing up to give a speech in front of the entire school? well... she'd accept her responsibilities but that sort of thing wasn't in her job description.

* * *

Hope you enjoyed this preview! "**A Deadly December in Edgemont**" is available in eBook, paperback, and audio. Find it at your favourite bookseller.

Also by Della North

Village of Edgemont
A Deadly December in Edgemont
A Fatal February in Edgemont
A Sinister Spring in Edgemont
A Crimeless Christmas in Edgemont

Standalone
Village of Edgemont Cozy Mysteries

Watch for more at dellanorth.ca.

About the Author

Della enjoys mysteries that won't keep her up at night, have a hint of romance, and a satisfactory ending. Preferably in a series.

She and her partner live with a tuxedo cat in the sunniest city in Canada, nestled in the foothills of the Rocky Mountains.

In November of 2022 Della undertook the National Novel Writing challenge to complete a 50.000 word first draft and the Village of Edgemont series began.

Books in this series:

1 - "**A Deadly December in Edgemont**"

2 - "**A Fatal February in Edgemont**"

3 - "**A Sinister Spring in Edgemont**"

Available in eBook, Paperback, or Audio.

Also *bundled-to-save* in the "**Village of Edgemont Cozy Mysteries Books 1-3**" collection.

A portion of sale proceeds will be donated to NaNoWriMo.org in appreciation.

Read more at dellanorth.ca.